First U.S. edition 1992
First published in Great Britain in 1992 by
Walker Books Ltd., London.
ISBN 1-56402-076-2
Library of Congress Catalog Card Number 91-58732
Library of Congress Cataloging-in-Publication Data
Cartlidge, Michelle.
Good night, Teddy / by Michelle Cartlidge.—1st U.S. ed.
(A Candlewick toddler book)
Summary: After playing in the bath, Teddy goes to bed
with his favorite toys.
ISBN 1-56402-076-2 : $5.96 ($7.95 Can.)
[1. Bedtime—Fiction. 2. Teddy bears—Fiction.]
I. Title. II. Series.
PZ7.C249Go   1992   91-58732
[E]—dc20

10 9 8 7 6 5 4 3 2 1

Printed in Hong Kong

Candlewick Press
2067 Massachusetts Avenue
Cambridge, Massachusetts 02140

Good Night, Teddy

by Michelle Cartlidge

CANDLEWICK PRESS
CAMBRIDGE, MASSACHUSETTS

Teddy loves to play
with his toys, but soon
it's time for bed.

"Bath time!" calls
Mommy Bear. Teddy
takes his sailboat,
his duck, and his
favorite Pink Rabbit.

Teddy sails his boat
and Rabbit watches
from the chair.
"Don't forget to
wash, Teddy," says
Mommy Bear.

Teddy dries himself,
then he brushes his teeth
and is ready for bed.

Elephant, Mousey, Moley, and Pussycat live in Teddy's bedroom. But where is Pink Rabbit?

Here comes Mommy
Bear. Look, she has
Pink Rabbit!
"Teddy, you left him
in the bathroom."

Teddy tucks his toys
in his bed. But is there
any room for Teddy?

"Goodnight, Teddy," whispers Mommy Bear, "and dream sweet dreams."